THE MUSTARD SEED

JODI LYNN

ILLUSTRATED BY SHENG–MEI LI

The Mustard Seed
Copyright © 2021 by Jodi Lynn

All rights reserved. No part of this publication may be reproduced, distributed, or transmitted in any form or by any means, including photocopying, recording, or other electronic or mechanical methods, without the prior written permission of the author, except in the case of brief quotations embodied in critical reviews and certain other non-commercial uses permitted by copyright law.

Tellwell Talent
www.tellwell.ca

ISBN
978-0-2288-5355-8 (Hardcover)
978-0-2288-5353-4 (Paperback)
978-0-2288-5354-1 (eBook)

The kingdom of heaven is like a mustard seed,

which a man took and planted in his field.

Though it is the smallest of all seeds,

yet when it grows,

it is the largest of garden plants and becomes a tree,

so that the birds come and perch in its branches.

Mathew 13:31-32

A story...

I want to tell
of my beautiful baby boy

and a seed
that made me well

medicine

for my soul.

The day I gave birth
to my handsome little one
I was filled with delight, mirth

and exceeding love

So joyful - so proud!

each day a new surprise

and I would laugh out loud

    at his blue
                  mischievous eyes.

Even so...
you shall see my story
becomes grim for I was met
with tragedy
        my life's light grew dim.

One tragic night
        he was taken

to illness, he did
                fall

to my depths, I was shaken...

the night death came to call.

Dear reader, please appreciate

my love

so raw... so wild

do not underestimate
the love I had for my child

I bundled him in blankets
and I held him tight.

Death's stony glare
 I would not meet
in the darkness of that night.

Crazed with pain
           I
            s
             t
              u
               m
                b
                 l
                  e
                   d

as if stabbed with a knife

in grief's fiery pit
           I fumbled

to bring my son back to life

There I stood, my grief wild, savage, unbroken
weeping for, my lost child

love's tender words unspoken.

It seemed my heart would fail
from sorrow and despair
in darkness I did wail

this grief, I could not bear

This man tried to console
he knew my son was dead
he saw the sickness in my soul

he took my hand and said,

dear woman, let me help you
I know a wise man
he will tell you what to do
and you'll be well again

We found this man quite easily
behind a large crowd
I strained my eyes to see

then I screamed out loud

*Teacher! Teacher!
look at me
I am frail and I am weak*

please, cure my baby

give me the medicine that I seek!

Then the crowd made way
for they were aware
the tragic cause, of my dismay...
my dead son lying there.

This teacher knelt beside me
he saw my son had died
I was sobbing on my knees
I met his eyes and cried

My son
the love, of my life
his laugh - his toothless grin
oh why could I not keep him safe?

Bring him to me again!

With quiet eyes

he saw me

with love
and gentle care

he looked upon my tragedy

my dead son lying there.

Then he said

*You did well
in coming here to me
and as far as I can tell
I have the medicine you need.*

Yes, dear one, you will find

the medicine you seek

but before I can, save your child
           please do something for me.

*A mustard seed, you must find
from any home, widespread
where no, loved one has died.*

with urgency he said

*Go now! Make your rounds
do not be denied
go until you've found
a seed from which none has died!*

Now, hope was in my heart...
would my son come back to me?

With faith, I did start
to find that magic seed!

I rushed to a family
I knocked upon the door
a kind woman greeted me
and I did implore...

I need some special medicine
for my beloved son
a tiny grain, a mustard seed
do you have one?

She said, *yes... a mustard seed*
no cause for concern
I can find one easily

then I recalled the teacher's words...

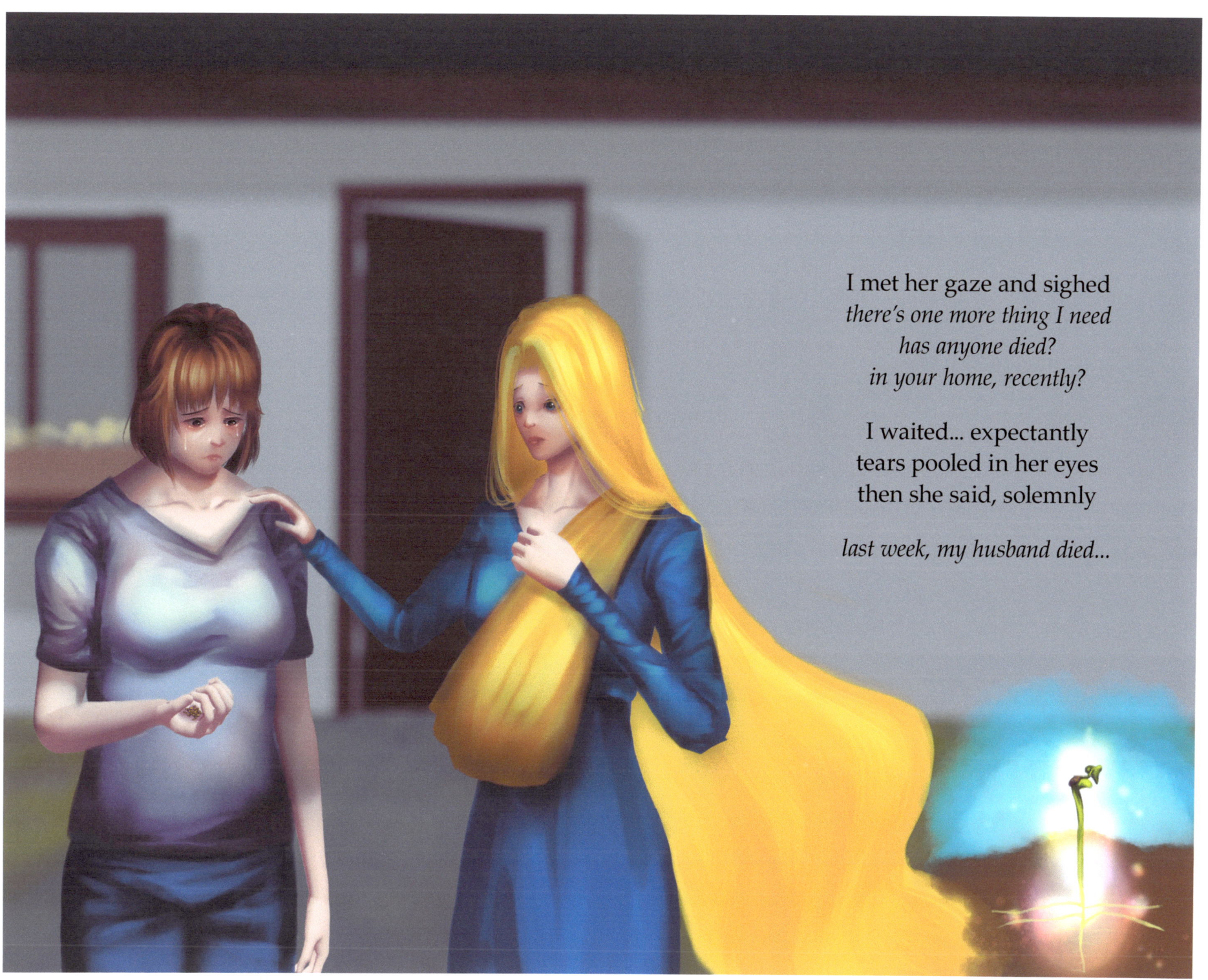

From house to house I went
not one I came across
at last, I was spent...

for all had suffered loss.

Like an unwelcome guest
death greeted each one there
and the gifts that he left

were heart-wrenching despair

I sat down and wept
and began to understand
each house I visited

was touched by death's
          sad
             hand

I gazed down at my son
cradled at my breast
in every home there were none

death's glare had not been met

Then, I went back to him
that master once again
not as sad as I had been

I looked at him and said

*Teacher, I could not find
that special mustard seed
in every home, someone has died
I can't give you what you need*

But I suspected
the master there

he knew

that magic seed he'd planted
in tenderness

it grew

Then, I wrapped my baby
to him I said goodbye

my heart was hurting
heavy

and tears streamed from my eyes

Now, dear reader
           please accept
love's tender seed
  loss has touched
           do not forget
all of humanity.

The medicine I sought
to heal my grief and pain
was the medicine he brought
to make me well
again.

www.ingramcontent.com/pod-product-compliance
Lightning Source LLC
LaVergne TN
LVHW071733060526
838200LV00032B/490